Visions
of my other self

Visions
of my other self

A NOVELLA

THOMAS TIMMINS

Zoëtown Media
Haydenville, MA

ISBN 978-0-9970287-4-4
Printed in the United States of America

Published by Zoëtown® Media
Zoëtown is a registered trademark of Zoëtown Media.
Haydenville, MA
www.thomastimmins.com

Cover photograph "Milky Way" Shutterstock
Book and cover design by Maureen Moore, Booksmyth Press
www.thebooksmythpress.com

*To you who've seen other worlds
without understanding them at all*

Visions of my other self

Rain

My hunt begins after rain... water surges and gurgles through the woods...the noise of rain dripping from leaf to leaf to leaf to earth protects me...I have no knife...mother's calming voice surrounds me...it's hard to see through fog...the blood of drowned animals is trying to rise into the sky, resisting rain that wants to smother fine blood back into the soil, forcing it deep underground...the path is sticky, but firm under my toes...

Path

Flakes of quartz stuck in the path catch pieces of crimson afternoon as rainwater washes trees clean of dust and yellow light...there is a settlement of abandoned cellars, barn walls, stone fences near here...I remember...red and orange rust from the old car puddles in front of my every step...steel surrendered to wet air flows over my feet, staining them the color of fire...a Model T pickup tilts into the ditch...its ragged fenders drizzle amber chips...

Shadows

Stretching away from their mothers in the afternoon mist, huge flat shadows of stumps begin tossing up and down little shadows of leaves and cobwebs... some of them snap free, zinging by my head while I keep a sharp lookout, hiking farther into places I've never seen...shadows swirl around me, trying to enter me under my fingernails and roots of my hairs...it tickles...I hear them scratching...

Frogs

Like iron, trees' great trunks hold up a gray bridge
of sky overhead...leaves are black and brittle on the
ground...my feet find the path through sharp leaves
when my eyes don't look...I follow my feet...a few
steps behind me the path disappears...frogs scramble across high ground on the invisible trail...mist is
thinning...I'm crossing a log over a stream...I've got to
find him soon...he doesn't live so far in the woods I'll
get lost from the farm, I hope...my other self drags a
branch across the trail behind me...

Ridge

He said I'd find him if I just keep going...the last time I saw him might have been years ago...he surprised me when he came up behind me from the east on the bare ridge above the farm...he said I should visit him whenever I wanted...this is the ridge trail isn't it?...he must know I'm looking for him...this must be the same way I used to go...this looks like the same stream...

Fog

Birds slip between great trees carrying off wreaths of fog in their beaks...saplings sprout around me now, their dense branches hung with blue moss and white and yellow scarves...the ground in the distance glows...crisp air slants up my nose...I breath out warm air...catching my breath like cotton in a colored bag, my other self strikes matches...candles in the fog...the glowing path dims...

Smoke

My other self cries out in her crow voice, more wind in it than snarl...from somewhere, there, off to my left...he sits there in the clearing, in a grassy bowl at the bottom of the hill...he's smoking, watching me...a tall hat of smoke rises around his head...where's your brother, he asks me...he gets up from his rock chair...where's your shining stone house I say...maybe my brother is there I say...maybe your brother is there he laughs...

Rumble

Growls and rumbles come out of the earth...boulders
holding up the hill shake and bounce...my body stays
still...I don't feel anything...he throws me his pipe...I
catch it...noise like a big lake ripping apart...

Dew

Dense fog clouds splash into the clearing...cold mist rises up under my pant cuffs...little birds swoop down from a clear sky...their mouths pop open...black oily drops slide off their tiny tongues...more fog rises around us...lets go inside your house...follow me he says...

Hill

Under my feet the trail uphill slips and shudders...
the hill shakes...his smoke stinks in my nose...the hill
shakes like a fat belly...the boulders are laughing....

Bridge

I clutch steel cables while my legs ride wooden waves
across the river...he's ahead of me jumping up and
down on the suspended bridge...when the waves peak,
he howls and jumps...my legs are too stiff...I can barely stand...I pull myself across in short steps...rippling
bridge jerks my neck back and forth...my head falls
off behind me, smashing into the planks...I slip into a
trough between the boards and my head bounds back
onto my neck...he's standing on the other shore shak-
ing the bridge...it rocks and shudders...it rolls up at
my face...my legs shrink...bridge falls away...glued to
the planks, my legs stretch down to the water...I land
on the shore breathless as a fish...

Clouds

Trucks and cars idle in front of a tilted barn...people stack hay in the beds of the trucks...as soon as they turn around for more, the hays blows away...dozens of people swarm the barnyard...boiling gray cumulus descend...children twirl in the blowing hay with hands in front of their faces...hay funnels into the clouds... the cumulus leans against the barn, shouldering the fences, kneeing the trucks and cars...I barely see the barn...clanging a hatchet against a hubcap, my other self marches in and out of the fog...barn dogs follow her, rubbing themselves against her legs like cats...

Slice

He hands me the knife, the knife with the blade taped to a wooden handle...it's heavy...I turn to the boar hanging dead from a rafter in the barn...a thin stream of bloods splatters in and out of a pan...the pan sits on a stove, the blood bubbles...my hand rises...I step back from the pig's body but my hand raises the knife, slashing down into the pig's belly...the sharp blade slices fat, slowly, sweetly, spreading fat like unzipping pants...rip through those chest bones he says...then swing him around and saw his head off...be careful of those guts...we want em whole...I carve away a square of fat as wide as my back dropping it into the pan of simmering blood...let's eat he says...everyone comes to the fire in the pit...only my other self retreats to the empty hayfield...she examines the clouds...they're flying away into the night....

Father

Climb up on the roof with me...hood the snout on your blade, toss it up here...I'll teach you to make a snout whistle...I came here to do what he tells me...he straddles the peak of the roof...someone shouts...horses whinny in pain...black chickens flock around the foot of the ladder I'm halfway up...my father stands up one leg on either side of the peak...he twists toward me, yelling for the snout...I toss it underhanded up to him...he lunges toward it, tipping off the roof...he falls down headfirst...I watch him slide past me, drop off the edge of the barn...I take off my boots...chickens flutter up to where my father was...black next to the weather vane...one chicken lands on my shoulder, pecks my ear...

Whip

My father picks himself up out of the pot of pig's blood...he rips my shirt off to wipe his face...he lifts me up...holding me like a plate, he carries me into the barn...dark except for the door, the barn whistles a low cow-mewling song...that's the snouts I saved from last winter my father whispers...a beautiful woman, a woman so beautiful my throat and face turn to wet straw when I look at her...her face is peaceful and brown...arms covered with brown fur...I can see through her glass hands to her white dress...she shrinks as she approaches...a whip not in her hands coils around her feet...it uncoils and coils again as she walks...the whip crawls to my feet coiling around my ankles...she picks it up by the thick end...the brown woman smiles at my father...his red lips open wide... she cracks the whip inside my father's mouth...he closes his eyes, leans back, nods...

Children

Chain necklaces ring the children's necks...someone holds an invisible leash attached to all of them...the children run as fast as they can, hurling themselves at the fence...their bodies jerk in mid-air, flopping to the ground...they lie still... a woman wearing a feather mask, rubies and diamonds shimmering down her long arms circles them...she sticks fat lighted candles in the kids' hair...red and purple and yellow green wax tears pool around the children's heads...an odor of vanilla and cinnamon rises over the foul barnyard...

Legs

I can't find him in the dark ahead of me...he's running
so I can learn to ride he says...I hear him cracking
sticks and grunting...stones roll down the hill, bounc-
ing off the stumps...wet pieces of stone spatter my
face...I pick slick, yellow stones out of my hair...they
might be my father's teeth...I follow the trail of blood
my father's legs leave for me...his legs might bleed
all night but he won't stop running...I climb straight
up...someone's house emptied itself onto the trail to
guide me through the night...I grab spokes of broken
wagon wheels and hoops of old bedsprings and fluted
poles of bent floor lamps and the pearly handle of an
empty refrigerator door to pull myself along...

Ships

On the other side of the hill, a blue light gleams out of trees...it is the sea's spirit risen to taste the dry world...I look down on the harbor with its few small ships...I'm exhausted, breathing sea light like water...I fill my lungs quickly and cough it out easily...I won't drown... the wind is fierce, driving pine needles through my shirt into my back...my father stands silently behind me...I smell blood on him, his mixed with pig's...

Hawk

Flooding past his eyes, shimmying under his neck feathers, wind gashes his wings...my eye is a grain of sand stuck to his beak...he floats on the wind swells... my eye screams, diving down faster than I've ever flown...this hawk is young and reckless...he slams into the wind over the bog behind the bay...frogs swarm, covering themselves with black water...the red hawk drops...my eye goes blind under water...

Slide

The wind, or my father, shouts, pushes me hard in the back...my feet fly up...they pull me downhill...my back slides over rocks and roots...my feet in the blue air drag my body straight downhill...I try to twist and turn myself loose...my back slides out of control through sharp dirt and hard rocks...my other self whirls around the hilltop holding hands with my father...they laugh and kick up their legs...light splashing up turns them orange...

Ragdoll

I try to hang on to the railing but the posts come loose...my head smashes stair after stair...I don't feel pain, just the jolting...my shoulders turn into soft clay...slivers pierce my skin but I don't bleed...I can hear animals watching...my voice cries my father's name...a sliver sticks out of my forehead with his name flashing on the point...my voice grabs my green eyes in its arms and leaps up into the sky...my eyes watch my body flopping like a sleeping ragdoll down the stairs...my voice drops anchor in a small gray cloud over the harbor...blue raindrops stain the buildings and streets below...my voice rattles windows with its laughing...my body drums down the mountain...cymbals crashing pour into my head through my empty eye sockets...

Fish
Big men wearing black boots toss fish up on the pier...
children pitch the fish back at the men...old women
hanging sheets and blankets laugh and snap wet
towels at the kids...I walk out on the pier, crossing
between the women and children...everybody's skin
looks shades of gray, like pencil drawings on paper...
one of the fish hits me on the chest and drops to the
greasy planks...a boy says are you invisible...no he's a
porcupine laughs another...don't let him steal our fish
a woman says...the men climb up out of the boat...I
let myself down into a boat to sleep...

Girl

A girl with one arm comes out of the hut at the end of the pier...the boat knocks again and again against the creosote posts saying let me under the pier...I like the idea, a ceiling over my head tonight...I don't care if it leaks...a storm approaches...the girl takes my hand... wait here...she will come to see you soon...the floor of the pier vibrates under my knees with every crash of waves...the girl turns to leave...my golden hair rips out of my skull and flies up her empty sleeve...an oar appears in my hand...I lean on the oar like a crutch... the oar bends...

Seagulls

The red rope of sun on the water draws the pier away from the shore...my boat trails the pier, pulling us back toward the shore...the pier aims itself like an arrow between the setting sun and my boat that won't sail...the hut on the pier shrinks...its windows reflect thousands of crying seagulls flipping overhead like a school of giant minnows...the window flickers...

Osprey

Beside the osprey, I squat, waiting in her shadow...I try to wait like an osprey...watching everything...seeing everything...someone inside the hut shouts those are my cards you cheatin' bastard...the voice rings with whiskey and smoke...deal over then, crazy man...a woman's voice fills the air above the pier with love...sailors on land die for that love...steamy love that makes the sailors forget the roll of sea inside their legs and necks and stiffen like oars...I reach into the osprey's broad neck feathers, drawing myself closer to her heart...her back opens up to me...my fingers circle her heart...it beats quickly in my hand...my heart rises through my mouth and sits on my shoulder...the osprey's beak turns toward my heart...it shines like corn...the hut glows like a chunk of bark rotting in the night woods...

White light

Your mother is coming whispers the osprey's heart...
the window panes burst...light white as moonlight
bursts through the window, flowing into the night in
a wave coming right at me...I shove my heart back
into my chest, stand up with the osprey, on our toes...
the light blows over us like a gale...I can't feel air but
I feel light burn into my forehead searching for my
tongue...

Soaked

My eyes go white blind...I cling to the osprey...my lungs become gills fallen in love with light...my lungs pump hard, making love to the light in my chest...my heart screams...white water boils over my head...I lose my footing...find me osprey save me I moan...feathers sprout out of my fingertips...milky foam curls up my nostrils...my lungs sing, drenched in light...white hands emerge from the light like heavy clouds...the hands become a mouth kissing my chest...my lungs groan as the hands suck the light away... the gills shrivel and crack...my lungs drop into my stomach... all that is left in my chest is a dry wind aching...

Gale

My boat rips loose from the pier and pitches onto the shore...the boat dissolves, the boat becomes high waves crushing the shore...the boat smashes into the rocky shore with a roar of a whole forest falling at once over a cliff...boulders explode, waves crash high on land, splintering trees, ruining houses, dissolving visible earth...my knees can't hear the sea...kelp clean and slippery wraps my ears...my ears hear chiming inside kelp eggs, chiming sea breeze from the days of calm...sifting through seal bones lodged in trees...

Ice

Rafters overhead shudder and creak...shingles evaporate in the storm...ice builds up in the stalls of the shed where I hid from the light...pigs and turkeys and cows and raccoons and squirrels break through barn doors for shelter...wooden walls bulge inward...seams between boards swell like bruises bleeding freezing wind through the cracks...my body crams itself between a cow and a deer for heat...horses step on my feet, grinding them into the frosty floor...

Bears

Wind rolls out of the woods bloated with animals... rabbits big as sheep leap onto bulls' backs...roaring bears the size of boars hang by their legs from the rafters...deadly paws slice horse necks...frogs in packs attack roosters who slash back...amphibian blood blends with horse blood...all the animals including me shit in terror...my body climbs to the hay loft looking for a pitchfork to defend myself with...

Deer

Antlers bang against the hayloft floor...a herd of giant red deer shred the stall walls...dogs pierced by furious bulls' horns twitch in the bulls' faces, their dead teeth tearing at the bulls' muzzles...red deer mount cows and steers, thrusting them against the posts, ramming them into each other...howling...bawling... icy wind tearing flesh...feathers and fur blow into the hayloft...the barn staggers and leans into the wind to hold itself upright...

Bull

I lay in the mud in the corner, cowering...my eyelashes shear off in the wind...laughing white light floods the barn...all the animals moan...a twin-pizzled Angus bull with balls big as a sack of oats climbs a mare who screams and bucks...the bull pins her to the bloody floor, crushing her hips while he pounds... bull breath condenses into icy drops that pile over the mare's back...hundreds of eyes in the barn roll back into skulls...white light congeals in white eyeballs bulging from faces...torn off and broken legs and ears stumble over corpses...some tails on stiff bodies curve and swish...my body lurches up, seeking a way out...my blue eyes drop into my frostbitten hands...I raise the eyes high to find the path through the dying, stinking mess of animals...

Blue legs

I race down the pasture, tripping on mounds of grass, slipping on cow shit...I chase the girl...her blue legs drive like tractors pulling empty wagons...she throws off her coat...she tears of her elbows, sailing them back at me like bats diving for bugs...her blue legs crawl up the cottonwood at the field's end...I pick up rocks big as my fists...I want to knock her out of the tree...I see her legs but her feet and body and head fade into the leaves...hey you better look behind you she calls...I turn around to see black and yellow smoke rise out of the barn behind a curtain of rain...a small volcano erupts in the storm a mile away...howling dogs charge down the pasture...I climb up beside the girl...

Giggling
My black legs shake on the cottonwood branch...if you wait here you'll be safe unless the bears come back...she giggles...she swings from branch to branch using her tail and arms...my face is stuck to rivulets dripping down the bark...I drink...spiders crawl in my hair...I feel lucky...the dogs circling the tree smell like burned hair...they snap their heads back to cast their teeth up at me...they want to fish me out of the tree... their bones leap out of their skin...rib bones and jaws bay up at me...the dogs' claws scrape bark off the tree just below my toes...a thousand squalling starlings land in the tree shrouding me behind their black bodies and silver cries...

Dog food

She tosses down a finger...rearing back, she lofts her foot out as far as she can throw...dogs go crazy for the meat, soaring up and buzzing the tree like flies...turning to me with a knife, she cuts a hunk of my thigh for the dogs...this will keep them quiet while we escape she says...I slice blue muscle and a thin strip of white fat off her arm, but I can't hold on to it...it slips out of my bloody hand...flying dogs spear it out of the air and fall with it to the ground...good-bye she says...or follow me...if you want to love me...

Laughing

Blue legs dash ahead of the dogs...she taunts the pack, running it in circles...she bounces over their heads, flicking noses and rumps with her clawed toes, skipping away from vicious jaws...her whole body disappears into the lead dog's mouth...under the trees the other dogs lie quietly gnawing leg and skull bones... her laughing drizzles off cottonwood leaves around me like spring rain...the dogs drag their meat off into the shadows behind white trees...flies swarm around the dog's heads, humming...her voice laughs high above me...I can't see her, the branches are too dense...her voice drives the white light away...the air turns the dark blue of her legs...

Whips

Bees swarm through the tree, hissing warnings...they land on my face, stabbing me with their stingers... my tongue bulges like a dead man's, my eyes leak out their juice...I jump into the salt pond...my hands feel their fingernails peeling off...they cling, biting down hard onto soggy cottonwood roots...her whips slash down on my bloody fingertips...the metal tips split them down the middle...mice crawl out of the cracks in the bones...her whips swoop across the pond, seeking anything above the water, seeking my back to brand it like my father's back...white light returns, thudding into the water, working down the gaps she's driven into the water with her whipping, skidding down the faults in the water to the sandy bottom... the light lifts the water up on invisible jacks, opening doors in the old car rotting down there, sweeping out all the seeds of new water...I'm standing on the hood of the truck, clutching roots as the truck sways...the water rises over the pond's banks...she lashes it into drops of mist that drift away sleepily over the field...I vomit white light out of my lungs...I lurch into dry air, scooping breaths into my mouth with my shattered hands...a geyser of rotted fish and cow shit smells boils up out of the pond...

Osprey

The osprey drifts down from the sky, slides under me, rises...my naked belly burrows into the osprey's back...my face hugs her neck...she climbs the clean wind over the harbor...I shield my eyes, watching the earth pass away under her wings...my eyes fall asleep and dream they are clouds rising higher and higher into the day...

Body

I can't tell if my shredded fingers are feathers or fingers...my body floats in warm yellow light...my lungs hang off my feet like grocery bags...my lungs tremble like two hearts...they groan their freedom to the sky...without lungs, I breathe, I fly...

Purple bruise
We flew behind the cliff where the osprey nests...my eyes tunnel into the osprey's skull...they find her eyes and sink into them...she accepts them without blinking...through our eyes I watch shadows underwater shift into fish, flowers, sharp boulders that hold up our cliff...the silver moon edges through the pines behind us...my mother's heart is bruised...I felt it too... my mother's fear got stuck in my belly...I had to run away...the osprey lifted me up with the fear and carried it on her wings...sharp wind over the sea tore the fear away... I saw it fall in a trail of white light my mother's heart spilled...the moon's trail on the water clots into a purple bruise in the night...I hear something like strutting on the hill behind our nest...giant shadows strut across the field...it's you, at last, dancing on the wavy green grass...

Face

You pluck straws from your face like whiskers, one by one...you dig quartz bits out of your lips...you strip snow from your hair...rip metal clips off your fingers and toes...unbutton your fur belly...slip out of your mountain goat's feet...sparrows and grackles escape from the center of your palms...you hold your long breasts up to me, squirting pink milk...you squat, your pee showers the plantain leaves...taking my fingers, pulling them toward your head, placing them under your jaw, hooking them behind your chin bone...tear it off, you order...I pull away the bloodless beautiful face I dreamed of kissing and kissing and kissing... your true face smiles at me...the face I could never dream until now...I have known this face forever tho I've never seen it before...I sling the false face over the cliff...it splashes far below where the moon slips under the water like an old seal gone hunting...

Sobbing
I lay my face on your belly in green moonlight...you stroke my back with flower petals...my eyes close...my father's legs bleed down the handle of my mother's whip, reddening her hands with his thin pale blood... my blue heart drops down the dogs' throats like spit... smashed against a waterlogged tree, my boat splinters in the middle of a calm lake...my ears moan in my brother's salty arms...I lay on your round belly sobbing...

In your cave

Handing me a burl of oak hollowed and filled with fish soup, you wrap me in blankets...candles glitter deep inside the cave...shadows wither on smooth walls where you hung brown carpets and quilts... smoke gurgles against the ceiling...driftwood statues march along the walls, candles lighting their bare branches...stalactite whips hang like mosses from the shadows...you wind delicate silver chain around my ankles, ring my ankles with turquoise and silver bracelets...drape a braided silver necklace over my head...thank you I say but I want to go outside...I try to get up...you say you're welcome but you don't have to go anywhere...I'll get you everything you need...

Necklace

An oven emerges from the clay walls with kindling burning in it...I make my legs turn, unknown by her...they walk over to the driftwood statues...my feet slip on water she spilled on the packed mud floor... stretching my neck around like a turtle, I watch her... she looks my way... I see she has removed her brown eyes and strung them on a tight necklace she wears like a torc around her neck...her eyes bulge from the torc like amber, like melting rubies...yellow skull bones glimmer around her eye sockets...my legs try to edge away, sneaking among nooks and crannies and low grottoes...she offers me tea, seeing me with the eyes on her neck...

Night's end

Two golden coyotes stop at the cave's entrance to listen to us...she whistles to them through thick lips...they turn away...I forget them until they return dragging the osprey's body by her gray legs, limp claws...flies desert my scabby ankles and wrists, landing on the osprey's wet crushed skull...candle flames gutter in the coyotes' eyes...distant beacons that warn no one of the coming storm...I stare at them, trying to stay awake...

Knocking from underground

She stops talking...why?...all night her mouth has gushed words shaped like fish and eggs...why don't you talk I plead with her...now that she's silent, my arms and legs stiffen up, changing color from silver to gray...the veins in my arms bulge out like violet streams...my neck is scraped raw from my twisting against the exquisite necklaces she freshens for me every morning...she cleans out the scabs and hair and the slimy skin before she replaces it...I won't try to heal your neck now she says but I will when you're ready...what do you mean I say I'm ready now...We have to make sure the necklace is beautiful...I may have to sell it...this afternoon, when I stood, my knees turned to silver buttons...they locked like padlocks holding my thighs to my calves...I screamed and stamped on the cave floor...a boom echoed from the rock walls...I stamped again...I stamped ten times... an echo came...then ten echoes...I tired soon, sitting down in my chains and jewels, letting my trap hold me in the cave...later, without any stamping, the booms started up, echoes followed, my silver knees vibrated...some one is underground, knocking, trying to make me understand...

Irrigation

All morning she digs holes at the mouth of her cave...
her hair turns white...she hauls a wheelbarrow loaded
with her whips to the row of holes...I wonder why she
doesn't sweat in the sun...she stretches her arms wide
to embrace her whips...dozens of whips.... red leather,
black leather, buggy whips, riding crops with sharp
tails, long braided shiny brown whips with metal
tips...she pokes a whip handle in every hole, then she
tamps the dirt tight around them...she squats beside
every dry whip and pees...a puff of yellow steam rises
inn the sun beam around every whip...

Standing at the mouth

Children gallop past on horses and donkeys...sage-brush rolls by, squeezing between the barbed wire fence and the cave...the sun stops still on its perch above the skinless mountains in the south...I haven't seen her for days...I haven't seen her for weeks...I miss you...before she left she showed me a stream at the rear of the cave that trickles smoky water tasting like garlic...my fists leak pus and blood constantly...I stand at the mouth of the cave, the door to the outside world, hollering, moaning...

Secret home

You found me...I had waited a month, a season without dreams...my silver cuffs opened in your fingers like yawns...you ask me why I ran away...everyone was looking for me, you say...I don't believe you I say...At first I thought I'd found a new home, my secret home on the cliff...I look around the cave...the driftwood and the candles have sagged into heaps of pre-history on the cave floor...on the lip of stone in front of the cave, gleaming ivory seagulls perch...

Across the lake

Canoeing moon spoor, we find the campsite I abandoned last summer...when you came back I prom-
ised to show you everything that mattered if you let
me go, if you came with me...oaks rattle in the chill
breeze...my wrists ache inside their bands of scar...I
lived at this camp far longer than I'd expected...with-
out matches, without friction, I can start fire here...I
spit on wood, crackles of flame spit back...back to
back, our bodies lean into each other, pushing flesh
through flesh like water through water...we twist our
necks so we can kiss...somehow we lose touch...I saw
a circus once with people who pretzeled their bodies
like us you say...I unload jerky and cheese and choc-
olate from the pack...our canoe smolders under the
bushes, cooling off after our dash through the boiling
lake...my fingers touch your hair...they melt in crisp
water bubbling out of your forehead...

Spying

Someone drives a truck into the woods bushwhacking the old logging trail...we smother our fire with dirt as the truck growls closer and closer...it stops on the other side of the tiny inlet we camp on...a woman's voice begins trilling up and down music scales...she stands by the water, raising her head to the trees, opening her mouth like a baby bird...a man leans against the stump of a giant fir watching her...we lie on our stomachs under a hedge, arms around each other, spying on them...three yellow and white birds settle around the woman's feet...she doesn't see them or us...his eyes close against the pure moonlight on her face...she sings....

Emergence
Water begins to heave and swell...bloated bodies of fish and frogs pop out of the surface like white drops of hail raining up, back into the sky...the trunk of a rusted green car emerges in front of us, then the roof bulges out of the water and the whole car bobs and floats...a small boy wearing shorts and a sweatshirt clinging to him climbs out of the back window...he splashes toward the shore pulling a baby by the arm behind him...the man beside the tree lifts the baby up and hands it to the mother who holds it over her shoulder like a throw rug rolled up...she sings while the baby begins to cry...the dead fish and the frogs stink up the whole camp area...I rise but immediately sink to my knees in the mud...my other self stands up, grabs my collar, pulls me off the ground...

New leaves

My other self drags me back to our canoe...she stares and stares at me...her black eyes suck all the heat from my face...she knows me better than I know her, better than I know myself...I want her to stop staring and let me go back to my mother singing in the moonlight but she takes my head in her hands like she's going to kiss me...my ribs shudder...the cloud behind her head rolls away...in the moonlight, tiny new leaves sprout out of the trunks of trees and off the tips of branches shimmering overhead...I hear you call wake up come and eat it's getting cold...

Fog
The people in this town have muddy water in their
heads you tell me as you drive us up a steep hill...I
get a headache when I stay too long, like I'm holding my breath too long underwater...people talk with
their cheeks full of slush...outside the wind growls by
like the whine and buzz of a motorboat in fish ears...
the window is cracked...we follow a caravan of flatbed
trailers...diesel smoke invades the car and our noses...we climb through thick fog steaming off the lake...

Green flowers

He waits for us in the inn under the ancient stone bridge...his pigs follow him everywhere, snorting and squealing, nosing toward us as we cross over, jumping from rock to rock...don't stop you urge me with your fingers pushing the middle of my back...god, do those pigs smell bad you say...eat some of this then I say handing you an onion from my pack...you won't be able to smell anything...hurry up you tell me...in the inn, she filled bowls and bottles and pans with cut white flowers...she stands at the window in the shade of the bridge and remembers something...all the flowers in the vases are tinged with green...pick up a bowl of white flowers to smell them and they turn completely green in your hands...in minutes, all the flowers in the room become green...the walls and floors are made of glowing yellow pine...he passes by the window outside...peeking in he asks how do you like my collections...we have no idea what he means...

Naked children

The hammer stiffens my wrist...it wants to strike wooden pegs until they flame...the pale blue dock eases itself into the water like an old man...groans and creaks of pleasure wash off the planks...dogs and children scramble down shedding shirts and pants into the weeds along the shore...I need both hands and arms to raise the sledge hammer above my head...when I slam the iron sledge into the post driving it through shallow water into split rock under sand, the dock shivers rattling my foot bones, my shin bones with the recoil...naked children ignoring me, brush against me and they leap and cartwheel off the tilting dock...my skin blisters where they touch me...

Blood

Standing in front of the mirror, my brother shaves the beard off his neck...with the edge of his razor, he opens a vein under his jaw, catching the blood spreading like silt down his neck in a yellow sponge... my other self holds him from behind, placing her palms over his bare belly button...he leans back into her chest, smiling and gasping...the blood stops flowing...he squeezes the sponge into a glass...take this to my brother, he says, before he changes his mind... my other self carries the glass to the porch where I'm sleeping in the hammock...she tells me I have to wake up...I'm not ready I say...you have to or the blood will be too thick to drink...you brother says...

Meat
Too many people sit around the table, talking, talking...come on we're having a great time she invites me
gently...my other self is drunk...locked into my chest,
my neck won't move forward...I take off my watch and
pitch it toward the table in front of them, hoping that
will satisfy them...she reaches out from behind a pic-
ture of New York in the old days, snatching the watch
in flight...you keep this, we don't need it...she tosses
it back, underhand...it bounces off my palm...when I
bend to pick it up, tears I can't stop slide off my lips...
my other self laughs but comes over to me opening
her black silk blouse...she offers me her breast...I put
it between my lips, lap at it with my tongue...it's hot
and sweet...I gnaw slowly, twirling her nipple around
my gums...with the meat of her in my mouth sooth-
ing me, I stop fearing the people sitting around the
table...my other self and I enter the dining room...

Afraid

Riding old Sam his father's workhorse at a gallop into our muddy yard he lets the snorting horse knock our stone hitching post into mother's goldfish pond... you're not going to make a good impression on me that way Carl my mother calls from the upstairs window...my sister trips down the porch stairs and stops herself against old Sam's sweating neck...you know I don't have a horse Carl she says...you can ride behind me he tells her, lifting her up by her two hands... my mother climbs onto her green bicycle...let's go she says to me...you can't ride a bike mom I say...she reaches her hand to my face, slyly dropping something into my pocket...my other self hugs my mother, breathing little coos into her neck...

Inside my chest

I find your name in an old window box hanging down from the wall like a dry leaf off a plant... in the kitchen my other self bastes a roast...I leave my money and tools with her...I ask your brothers to leave us alone while we work on the tree house...your oldest brother shows us the tiny red symbols tattooed into his fingertips...it looks like dirt and grease worn in from fixing cars I tell him...you better not let me catch you he says threatening my other self with some punishment for letting my mouth run off so sassy...we swore we'd take care of her I said after her barn burned down so leave her alone...pressing one of her red tail hawk feathers into his hand I say watch out she might fly away...ha he laughs, track her down on the wind... you're inside my chest listening to me and my brother and my other self fooling around...you start to giggle...my throat itches with your laughing...

Road building

We stand in the ditch... he shows me how to stack rocks around the gap between the culvert and the road so the road won't fall in no matter how much traffic, no matter how many years...then he takes a hunk of salted meat from his pouch...plant this venison under this keystone...when the arch takes a mind to buckle a bit the meat will cushion it...he picks up my bag of tools and hangs them from the willow root behind me...he pulls his arms and legs off stacking them teepee style in the dry streambed...he tells me to pull his hair out and mount it up under his arms and legs for kindling...time to make a fire he says...it's almost dark...

Inside

My other self leaves the shade in the dry ditch...she
has to feed her skin sunlight or she loses control of
it...I've seen fat ooze out of her shoulders like sweat
in the dark...drawing me close you say my brothers
would love to meet your other self...they don't really
want to...they'd have to come inside and sit around
for hours...my hands peel away your sheepskin coat...
when you shrug your shoulders my invisible body
slips inside your clothes...rubbing against you I feel
rough cloth scraping my thighs and belly...the heat
rises up the flue between my invisible flesh and your
cotton shirt...

Digging

She comes out of the house at the end of the street, dragging her feet, then skipping, then dragging...I watch her through my eyelashes as she approaches me with her hands in her pockets...don't you think it's a little dangerous to dig holes where people are always running and playing she says...my other self starts to fill in the holes but I stop her...this is my property I say...whatever I find in the ground is mine to keep...I'm in my yard digging so if bones break they're my bones...my other self fills in a hole...she turns her pockets inside out...coins and keys spill out...laughing, she plants them in the holes...

Notes

I hear my sister playing the piano...the music cuts through webs spiders made in the bushes eating flies and roaches...while the Bach eats insects I sneak up on it, trapping notes between my fingers...I pretend the notes are tiny people and wild animals...I lay under the bushes playing cowboys and Indians in Africa...when my sister stops playing, the notes turn into little soldiers with long guns and bazookas hot as embers in my hands...

Leap

She tells me to leave...your sister is too old for me
now my other self says...if you want to build the
house of your dreams she can help you but you have
to go home now...I take back the sweater and blanket
I brought over this morning...my other self holds out
a plate with a sliced loaf of bread and a long serrated
knife on it...I take the knife as my reward...leaving
the bread I turn around...I'm on the far hill leaping
out of my other self's skin...ignoring me she crushes
her leg bones into fine powder and sprinkles it over
the mountain paintbrush...she can do whatever she
wants...

Silent language

We're underwater swimming in the deepest part of
the lake...the icy inlet is hot this year...lakeweed dan-
gles in the lit water snarling the hooks of our toes and
fingers...my ears become gills again...your arms are
fins...we speak to each other in the silent language of
currents...

Near hill

I'll meet you at dusk to answer any questions you still have he tells me while I'm digging the drainage ditch below the new house...all my questions don't matter now I say hefting boulders...I lie down in the sun to listen for his whistle while my other self splashes in the silty drainage water...she can't resist water anywhere, any time...look at those orange snakes...they have legs like centipedes...do you think they're poison...I'm on the near hill crawling toward the house when I hear the faint whistle from far upstream...I'm too tired, I say...I tell my other self you go...

Listening

The farm grew gathers and clambers up and down the barn scaffolding all morning...my mother wails in the graveyard wandering, stubbing her toes on gravestones...I'm on the roof listening...bolts rattle in the weather vane as it shudders on top of the cupola...I hear my other self pulling her new feet out of the ground...she crunches insects and snaps bulbs under her bare heels...

Shortcut

If you want to climb the ledge where roses can grow in winter I know where it is you say...teasing me with your fingernails scratching lightly across the back of my neck...my other self knows the way too I say so we can stay here for now if you want...but he's waiting for us you say it's a surprise...I didn't want to tell you but if you really don't want to go I'll go alone you say... angry you slam the door open and leave...I find my rifle and load it...I take target practice until my other self shows up...she takes me to the shortcut over the ruined bridge...

Heart

The osprey sails down to the rocky beach where I sit in sea mud, piling stones...she drops me a burlap bag that bounces on the rocks...I open the bag to find small fish and brass coins...she lands and invites me to lean against her breast while I eat...I smell dried blood on her beak...fur clings to her talons...my other self climbs on the osprey's back...they rise quickly toward the osprey's nest in the pine...bring the fish home for dinner my other self calls...tomorrow is the last day of sunlight for a week, remember...I barely hear my other self...the beat of the soaring osprey's heart drums in my ears...